THIS WAY UP

AIR MAIL

D1514953

For Phil, Lori, and Jamie.

First edition for the U.S. published in 2011
by Barron's Educational Series, Inc.

First published in Great Britain in 2011 by
Simon and Schuster UK ltd.
1st Floor, 222 Gray's Inn Road
London, WC1X 8HB.

Text and Illustrations copyright
© 2011 Richard Byrne.

All inquiries should be addressed to:
Barron's Educational Series, Inc.
250 Wireless Boulevard
Hauppauge, New York 11788
www.barronseduc.com

ISBN-13: 978-0-7641-4685-5
ISBN-10: 0-7641-4685-8

Library of Congress Catalog Card. No.: 2010935863

Date of Manufacture: December 2010
Manufactured by: Leo Paper Products, Kowloon, Hong Kong

Printed in China

9 8 7 6 5 4 3 2 1

Product conforms to all applicable CPSC and CPSIA 2008
standards.
No lead or phthalate hazard.

Millicent
and
MEER

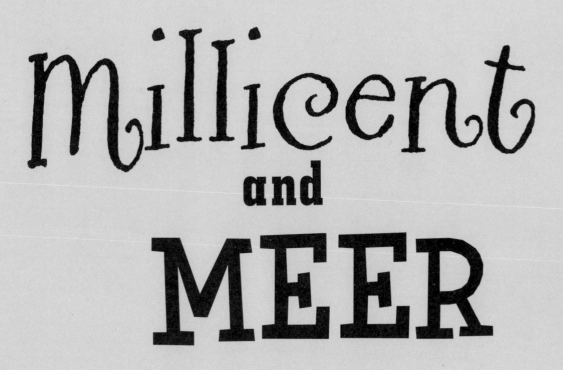

Richard Byrne

BARRON'S

One Saturday, **Millicent** was busy
making **sand castles** in the garden

when . . .

THUMP!

A big wooden box landed beside her.

"Ouch!" said the big wooden box.

Millicent peeped under the lid.

A dazed-looking **creature** sat inside.

"Hello in there. Are you OK?" asked Millicent.

"Hmm, I think so," replied the creature, rubbing its head. "But I've got no idea who I am or how I got here."

Millicent giggled. "You're **funny.** Perhaps I can help?"

Millicent spotted a label on the big wooden box.

"Mm . . . ee . . . er . . . ka . . . t.

Mystery solved!" said Millicent.
"You're a cat and your name is Meer.

Yippee!

I've always wanted a cat. You can be MY cat."

She took Meer inside.

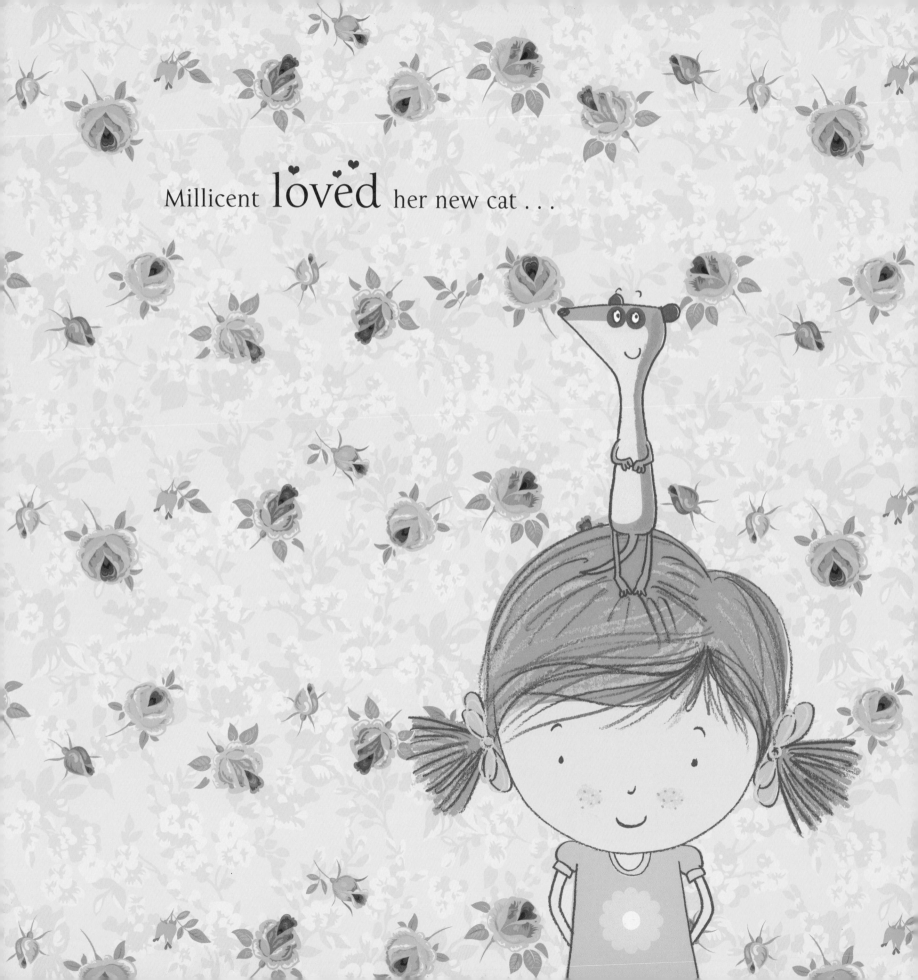

Millicent **lŏvĕd** her new cat . . .

. . . but he did do some
very **uncatty** things.

And some very **naughty** things, too!

Millicent's dad got **angrier** and **angrier**.

"**THAT'S IT!**" he said.
"Meer will have to go outside until he can learn
to behave like a **proper** cat."

Millicent didn't like putting Meer outside.

And Meer certainly didn't like **being** outside.

Poor Meer had been sitting all alone for some time when a stray cat came strolling past.

"Hey, why the sad face?" the cat asked.

"I have to stay outside until I can learn to behave like a **proper** cat," Meer explained.

"**Well**, you don't look like much of a cat to me, but today's your lucky day. **Marvin's** the name and being a cat is my game. Just follow me."

Being a **proper** cat was a little tricky at first.

But Meer soon got the hang of it.

Then . . .

WOOF! WOOF!

"Dog! Quick! Run!" cried Marvin.

Meer wasn't sure what a dog was but he was sure that he didn't want to find out!

Marvin and Meer ran and ran until . . .

. . . something caught Meer's eye.

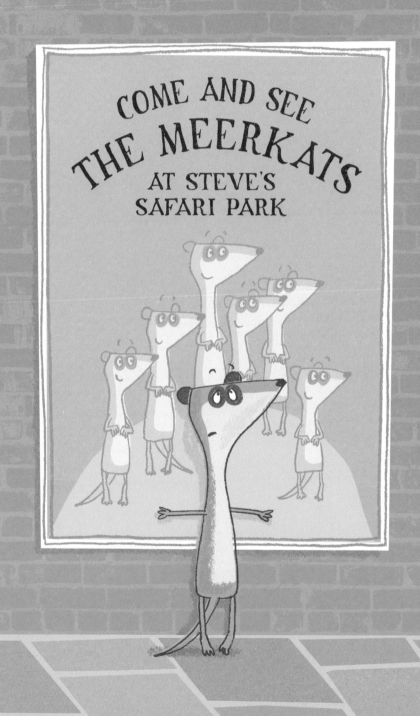

"Nice move, Meer. We've lost him. Now that was clever, even if you're NOT a cat," said Marvin.

"I'm not a cat?" replied Meer.

"No, look, you're a MEERkat!"

Marvin and Meer showed Millicent what they had discovered.

"So Meer isn't a cat doing **naughty things.**
He's just a meerkat doing **meerkat things,"**
said Millicent.

"That explains everything," said Dad. "But it's
not fair to keep Meer here. He belongs at the
safari park with the rest of his family."

Later that day, a van arrived to take Meer back to his family.
Millicent and Marvin waved goodbye.

They were **really** going to miss Meer.

"Are you going home to your family too, Marvin?" asked Millicent.
"I don't have a home . . . **or** a family," sighed Marvin, sadly.

"Yippee!" said Millicent.

"I've always wanted a cat. YOU can be my cat!"

She took Marvin inside.

Millicent and Marvin did lots of **fun things** together.

Millicent loved her new pet.
And Marvin loved his new home.

But, **best of all**, every weekend they went to the safari park
and did lots of meerkat things with Meer and his family!

WELCOME TO
STEVE'S
Safari Park

THE END